The Adventures of
YOO-LAH-TEEN

THE ADVENTURES OF
YOO-LAH-TEEN

A Legend of the Salish Coastal Indians by

ELLEN TIFFANY PUGH

Pictures by Laszlo Kubinyi

The Dial Press  *New York*

Library of Congress Cataloging in Publication Data
Pugh, Ellen, 1920–
The adventures of Yoo-Lah-Teen.
1. Salishan Indians—Legends. [1. Salishan Indians—Legends.
2. Indians of North America—Northwest, Pacific—Legends]
I. Kubinyi, Laszlo, 1937–   II. Title.
E99.S21P83   398.2'09795   75-9199
ISBN 0-8037-6318-2   ISBN 0-8037-6319-0 lib. bdg.

For the Sones family:
Pat and Bob,
Ted, Loralei, Mike, Marc, and
—of course—Ricky

FOREWORD

A little more than a hundred years ago a missionary lived and worked among the Indians of our great Pacific Northwest. No one knows what church he represented or even his name. All we know is that he was fascinated by the legends and tales of the Coast Salish Indian tribes and wrote some of them down in detail, in English.

In about 1897, as he was crossing Puget Sound alone in an open boat, a storm came up, the boat capsized, and he drowned. When his body washed ashore, the few sheets of rolled paper upon which he had written the tales were found in a sealskin pouch tied about his neck. Now, crumbling and with the ink barely legible from the passing of time, they have come at last to rest in a college library in the area.

There some months ago I happened upon them. And from them I have chosen the adventures of Yoo-lah-teen to retell. I have kept as close to the unknown missionary's manuscript as I could and still have the story easy to read and understand.

Specialists in folklore are interested in this authentic native American legend because of its echoes of the age-old classic tales of Hansel and Gretel, Jack the Giant Killer, and Jack and the Beanstalk.

The ordinary reader will, it is hoped, find the legend interesting for its own sake.

E. T. P.
Pullman, Washington
February 1975

CONTENTS

The Adventures of
YOO-LAH-TEEN

I

THE WITCH
APPEARS

They called her Ish-me-ooth. Tall she was, twice—no, three times as tall as any human and half as high as the giant trees that grow on the islands in Puget Sound, in the great Pacific Northwest. In the exact center of one island, in a clearing in the deep forest, she had her dwelling-place. But she was only in it at night, for all day long, every day, Ish-me-ooth went searching—searching for children. On her back she carried a great basket into which she flung those she caught. The thin ones became her slaves; the fat ones she roasted over an open fire, then feasted upon them.

It was true that no one had ever actually seen Ish-me-ooth, but the six tribes of Salish Indians who lived on the big island knew she was real. As real as the ogre Nuck-ah-too, who was her lover. They knew this though they lived entirely on the shore; for until Yoo-lah-teen came none dared venture into the dark interior of the island. Evil forces lurked there.

One early spring morning in the Moon of Greenness Come Again, seven children played on the beach in front of their village. The tide was out, the gray-green water dotted with whitecaps that ran before a north wind. Above the lapping waves a few gulls coasted on the chill air. Laughing and shouting, shoving one another about teasingly, the five little girls and two boys moved farther and farther away from home.

There was so much for them to see and do! First they followed the zigzag tracks a great blue heron had printed on the hard wet sand. Then they watched a moon snail move back very slowly to his shell and pack his too-big self into it. They came upon an exposed rock and examined all the living things clinging to it: barnacles, thin-shelled blue mussels, a spiny sea urchin, and a blood-red starfish. They were so busy none of them noticed that the three longhouses of their village were out of sight.

Ebb tide had left smooth, brightly colored pebbles scattered over the beach, and the children fell to gathering them, shouting with joy at each new find. Suddenly two girls reached for the same yellow pebble.

4

"I saw it first!" the older girl exclaimed. "It's mine."

"It's not!" said the other, whose name was Pay-koh, closing her fist over it.

"Give it to me," the first one demanded.

Pay-koh danced out of reach. "You can't make me. Just because you're almost eight, while I'm only seven . . ."

The older girl followed her. "Give it to me or I'll . . . I'll call Ish-me-ooth to come get you!" she said. It was the worst threat she could make.

Pay-koh stared at her companion. "You wouldn't dare!" she taunted. Then, a mischievous smile on her face, she dashed into the Sound, scooped water with her free hand, and flung it straight at her challenger.

"I do dare," the older girl said, ducking the icy water. She squared her shoulders and tossed her head back. She had made the threat; she must now carry it through.

"Ish-me-ooth!" she called, not very loudly and with a tremor in her voice. Suppose—just suppose—the *chehah*, the evil witch, should come! But nothing happened, so she called again, louder this time.

"Ish-me-ooth! Ish-me-ooth! Come here!" Her words rang in the early stillness.

At once there was an answering sound—a weird screech that sent cold shivers chasing up and down the children's spines. They drew together, trembling, eyes wide with fright, as a monstrous figure came crashing out of the forest.

Draped in a dark, tattered blanket, she strode toward them. Sharp cheekbones stood out in her sunken face, and a long thin nose reached to her chin. Her eyes flashed red fire from deep, dark sockets. She pointed her long, gnarled walking stick at the children and, in an awful voice, cried, "Who calls me by my name? Who calls Ish-me-ooth?"

The children screamed, broke apart from one another and ran, tripping and falling in their eagerness to get away. But it was no use. With a single step the *chehah* could reach the farthest child.

Ish-me-ooth gave a fiendish laugh, dropped her stick, and pounced. With the long, sharp talons of one hand she snatched the first child she came upon—the girl who had called her. With the other hand she reached into a pouch tied at her waist and smeared a sticky gum, made from the sap of a fir tree, over the terrified girl's eyes. Ish-me-ooth was taking no chances on anyone peeking and learning the way to her lodge. Then the witch tossed her victim into the bottom of the basket on her back.

When Ish-me-ooth had captured all seven children, she cackled again, picked up her walking stick, and marched off into the forest.

The youngsters cowered together in the huge basket, hearts beating wildly, thinking only of the horrible fate in store for them when Ish-me-ooth reached her destination. But the *che-*

6

hah didn't stop. On and on she walked, ever deeper into the woodland.

Because she was so tall, Ish-me-ooth often had to stoop to pass under trees that had low-hanging branches. At such times the limbs would scrape the top of the basket. The children, though they couldn't see what was happening, could hear the rasping noise. This gave the two at the top of the heap an idea.

They nudged each other, not daring to whisper, and awaited their chance. Then, the next time they felt Ish-me-ooth bend over, they raised their arms quickly, grabbed hold of a sturdy branch, and held on tightly. The witch strode on, not noticing that her burden was a bit lighter.

When they were sure it was safe to do so, the girl and boy let go of the limb and fell unharmed onto the thick, spongy cushion of fir needles that carpeted the ground. With their fingers they clawed enough of the pitch from their eyes to be able to open them.

They looked about in wonder. How different this lush, green, enclosed world was from the open sea, sky, and sand of their beach home. But their interest dwindled when they realized they were hopelessly lost.

"How will we ever get home?" asked the girl, biting back her tears.

"I . . . I don't know," answered the boy. "But we must get away from here. The *chehah* will miss us and . . . and come back!" His voice quivered.

8

The two children rushed first one way, then another in their panic. Then suddenly they came upon a deep, swift-flowing stream. Kneeling, they drank eagerly.

"All of this has to go somewhere," said the boy half to himself, extending his arm in the direction of the water's flow.

The girl nodded. "Otherwise the forest would be flooded," she agreed.

"It goes to the ocean," the boy said firmly after a moment's thought. "It has to. All we need to do is follow it."

They laughed aloud in relief. Joining hands, they hurried on, for they had a very long way to go, and besides, the witch might come back at any moment! They stopped only a few times—to watch a startled doe nuzzle her new fawn, to breathe in the pungent aroma of leafmold, licorice fern, and wild ginger, and to listen to the rich, melting warble of a purple finch hidden somewhere in the arching treetops above them.

It was sundown before they heard the roar of the surf and came out onto the broad beach within sight of their own village. The stream that had been so deep and swift far back in the woods became the wide, slow-moving one from which the tribe got its fresh water.

Tired and hungry, they stumbled into their frantic parents' arms. As the two sobbed out all that had happened to them since morning, the villagers crowded around, listening in stunned silence. And the other five children! Seized by Ish-me-ooth! Nothing could be worse.

The mothers of those who had been taken turned aside and wept, while the fathers clenched their fists and shook with mixed rage and fear. Ish-me-ooth was real; they had always known that. Other tribes on the island had suffered such kidnapings, but now she had stolen their children. Perhaps by this time she had ripped them open with her giant hands and devoured them.

There was only one thing to do. First the Indians kindled a large fire on the hearth outside the lodge, piling the great cedar logs high. Then, as the stars came out, everyone joined in chanting the slow, mournful Song of Death. From time to time, as the fire died, a young man rose and poured precious whale oil on the live embers. The fire renewed itself, sending great sheets of orange-red flame skyward.

For four days and four nights the tribe sat ringed around the ceremonial fire, repeating the dirge. Then the Indians took up their regular daily life. The kidnaping was now taboo; never again would they speak of this awful event.

Weeks passed, and it was the Moon of the Leaping Salmon— a busy time for everyone. The men and boys trapped or speared the big fish, while the women and girls cleaned them with mussel-shell knives, stripped the flesh, and hung it on racks to smoke slowly over alder-wood fires. The dried salmon would be food for the winter months, when the roots and berries that grew in abundance at the edge of the forest were not in season.

With so much to do, the mothers of the missing children began to be comforted, to weep a little less over their loss. All except one, all except See-tum-kah. She sorrowed always and would not be soothed.

II

YOO-LAH-TEEN ARRIVES

At dawn each day See-tum-kah crept from the longhouse and walked along the beach. She was a short, stocky woman, and her full skirt of shredded bark swung rhythmically as she strolled. When she reached her favorite spot, she sat in the sand facing the sea. Most mornings now, in early spring, there was fog. She liked sitting wrapped in its moist gray blanket. It gave her a feeling of being all alone in the universe that accorded well with her grief.

Then, as the fog thinned and wan sunlight struck the waves, See-tum-kah prayed aloud to the *Sag-hal-lee Tyee*, the Great

Spirit who lived in the blue sky above, to care for her daughter's soul. Next she chanted the low, sad Song of Death:

> *For my child is dead*
> *While others yet live*
> > *Ai-ya-ya-yai.*
> *Come back, daughter, come back*
> *I miss you, I need you*
> > *Ai-ya-ya-yai.*
> *Come back to me, my lost one*
> *And be again all my joy*
> > *Ai-ya-ya-yai.*
> *Oh, dearest child, where are you now?*
> *Come back to me, my loved daughter*
> > *Ai-ya-ya-yai.*
> *Your death darkens the sun*
> *I am lonely*
> *I am sad.*

As she sang, she wept. The tears dripped from her chin onto the sand. One morning as she cried, she thought she saw a slight movement in the spot her tears had dampened. The next morning she was certain. Day by day the motion increased. Then the sand began to rise, making a tiny mound. "What can this be?" she asked herself. She thought about it all through that day, and the next, and the next.

Finally the morning came when, to her amazement, See-

tum-kah saw that the bit of tear-drenched sand had taken the form of a child. But a very small child—one no bigger than her little finger!

Wondering at this miracle, See-tum-kah searched the water's edge until she found a shell that was just the right size and shape to make a perfect cradle for the baby. Lining it with seaweed, she lifted the little figure from the sand and gently laid it in the shell's pearly curve. Still wondering, she carried it to the dark lodge, covered it with a piece of soft blanket she had woven from shredded bark and dog hair, and set it on the earthen floor.

Though still grieving for her lost daughter, See-tum-kah became more and more interested in the sand child. She spent hours staring down at the strange little body, its eyes closed in sleep. Sometimes she even sang lullabies to it.

Then one day, several weeks later, when she looked into the shell, it was empty! Her heart skipped a beat and cold sweat bathed her forehead. What could have happened? She stared all around—and then she saw him. Beside the shell, and no higher than her ankle, stood a boy—arms akimbo and smiling up at her.

Bending to the ground, See-tum-kah lifted him onto her hand and examined him carefully. Though so very small, his face and body were perfectly formed, and he was beautiful to look upon. He accepted See-tum-kah as his mother, and in that moment she loved him as her son.

The boy grew so fast that each morning See-tum-kah had to hunt for a larger shell to be his bed. Very soon, though, he stood as high as her knee and had no need of a cradle.

"What are you going to name him?" the curious villagers asked.

"Yes, how are we to call your son?" questioned the chief.

See-tum-kah thought many days before answering. Finally she told everyone, "There is only one name for him, and it is Yoo-lah-teen." The people nodded. It meant The Wondrous One.

And he was. In all the village there was no one like him. In a short time he was as tall as a boy of twelve. He could run faster than any other boy and could wrestle those who were twice his weight. On shore he could net more ducks and snow geese, and at sea he had no equal in the dangerous harpooning of porpoises and hair seals.

Naturally the other youths were jealous of his great ability and sometimes muttered against him. But Yoo-lah-teen was so good-natured that, try as they would, they couldn't dislike him.

The days passed pleasantly for the boy, except for one worry. His heart was troubled by his mother's constant sorrow. Yoo-lah-teen couldn't know for whom she grieved because no one ever spoke of it. But he saw tears in See-tum-kah's eyes whenever she looked toward the forest.

One soft summer evening in the Spiceberry Moon the boy and his mother sat together outside the lodge. Beside her lay a great pile of velvety, long-stemmed cattails. Before long the autumn rains would begin, and the people would need the waterproof capes she so deftly fashioned from the reeds.

Yoo-lah-teen, meanwhile, chipped arrowheads. At the edge of the woods *ol-lal-lee* bushes were ready to burst into snowy, fragrant flower. Deer loved both bud and leaf and came out of the forest at twilight to nibble them. It was the only chance the men and boys had to shoot the deer, since none of the Indians would go into the woods to hunt.

See-tum-kah and her son were silent except for her sighs. Occasionally she brushed away a tear. Yoo-lah-teen decided the time had come to ask about her sadness.

"Tell me, my mother," he began, "why it is you sorrow so. Have you lost a warrior brother? Do you still mourn your husband, six years dead? Why do you cry?"

See-tum-kah did not answer. It was forbidden to speak about it, but surely, to this strange young boy . . . ? Looking carefully about to make sure the others could not overhear, she whispered to her son the story of Ish-me-ooth and the seven children the witch had stolen.

"And one of the five who didn't come back was my daughter, Pay-koh. Though older than you, she would be much smaller than you are now, so I say it is for your little sister that I grieve," See-tum-kah said, weeping softly.

17

As he listened, Yoo-lah-teen felt his heart swell with rage at the *chehah* who had done this awful thing. He resolved that he, Yoo-lah-teen, would be the one to rid the world of this evil being.

"Mother," he said, "I am going to search for Ish-me-ooth and slay her. Perhaps by some chance my sister still lives. If so, I will bring her home to you."

See-tum-kah looked up into the darkening sky. Stars pierced the blackness in sharp, brilliant patterns that were reflected in the calm sea below—but blurred, out of focus, softened. Yet the beauty of the night could not dispel the alarm she felt at his words. She had lost her daughter; was she also to lose her son?

"The *chehah* will catch you, tear you in pieces, and eat you," she said, shuddering. "That is if the ogre, Nuck-ah-too, doesn't get you first! Oh, Yoo-lah-teen, you are so young yet. Stay here, where it is safe."

But Yoo-lah-teen only smiled. "I have no fear, Mother," he said quietly and stood up. "I must find the witch and destroy her."

At dawn Yoo-lah-teen left the lodge, clad only in his breechcloth, with a dried, hollow gourd encircling his waist. He carried no weapon—no whalebone club, no bow and arrow. These would be useless against the tremendous size and strength of the *chehah*. If it were true, as See-tum-kah vowed,

18

that he was a wonder-boy, born of her tears and the sand of the beach, he could not be harmed by any mortal. But Ish-me-ooth was more than human. He would have to rely on his own quick wits and nothing else.

With a new sadness See-tum-kah watched Yoo-lah-teen disappear into the dark and gloomy forest.

III

YOO-LAH-TEEN
SEARCHES
FOR THE WITCH

In the eerie half-light of dawn Yoo-lah-teen turned his face away from the wind-rippled sea. Without once looking back, he crossed the beach until he came to the edge of the woods.

Pushing his way through the head-high brush, he soon made his way farther into the forest than anyone else of the island tribes had ever been—except, of course, the unfortunate children who had been caught by the witch.

Here the giant trees grew so close together that only a little of the morning light filtered through. Yoo-lah-teen peered through the gloom in every direction, trying to see a path

20

that Ish-me-ooth might have taken. There was none. But somewhere in this great woods was her lodge, and he was determined to find it.

He hurried on, making no sound as his feet sank into the thick mulch of decayed leaves and needles.

The cool air was heavy with new, sweet odors—wild plum, osoberry, honeysuckle, and roses. And the forest was alive with bird songs. Black-and-orange towhees piped clear notes, scratching in the leaves at Yoo-lah-teen's feet. The chirping of linnets was answered by the high, tinkling trill of wrens. And everywhere summer swallows, violet-green, skimmed by on long, pointed wings.

Amazed at all he saw and heard, Yoo-lah-teen moved on, always searching for some sign of Ish-me-ooth's presence.

Suddenly a high, dismal, long-drawn-out howl made him stop short, quivering. Then he realized it was only *wah-wah-seek*, a timber wolf. He walked on.

Hours passed; the sun was directly overhead, the day much warmer. Yet the only big creatures he came upon were a cougar that dashed across his path and, in the distance, a black bear feeding on marsh lilies.

This reminded Yoo-lah-teen that he too was hungry. The Spiceberry Moon was one of the three Moons of Ripeness, so food aplenty was at hand. He had but to stretch out his arm, pick, and eat. First, he popped dark blue huckleberries into his mouth, letting the cool, luscious juice trickle down his throat.

Then he feasted on *kah-wee,* sweet blackcaps. Salal berries, with their rich purple color and spicy aroma, hung everywhere. Salmonberry thickets offered him their scarlet, hairy fruits.

Soon he was full to bursting but no nearer to Ish-me-ooth. Where could she be? He had come a very long way since morning.

He yawned and stretched. The warmth of the afternoon sun made him drowsy. A fallen log, blanketed with silky, yellow-green moss, invited him. He sank heavily onto it; he would rest just a moment.

He awoke with a start to the strange, deafening noise of a woodpecker just above him. Angry with himself for falling asleep, Yoo-lah-teen jumped up. The sun was much lower in the sky; he must hurry if he was to find the *chehah* before nightfall.

He plodded along for quite some distance, feeling the ground gradually rise. Soon he came to a broad clearing. Here the marshy earth was littered with moss-covered boulders. He threaded his way among them—frogs leaped from under his feet, croaking in protest.

Then he came to the edge of a cliff. Far below ran a wide, shallow river. He was about to clamber down and drink of its cool water when he glanced across to the far bank. He gasped.

There in the shadow of the forest stood a great wooden lodge, as large as all three longhouses of his village put to-

22

gether! Such a monstrous building could only be Ish-me-ooth's house.

Even as he stared, loud stomping noises came from within. Blue smoke was rising from the smoke-hole. She must be preparing her evening meal. Her meal . . . of children.

Yoo-lah-teen shuddered. He clenched his fists and started to climb down the bank. He was so angry he was ready to battle the witch with his bare hands, this very minute.

Then he reconsidered. Twilight was fading fast. In a very short while it would be night, and he would be unable to see well. Far better to wait until morning, for against the evil witch he needed every advantage he could get. Also, he had much to do to prepare himself for the combat. Yes, he would wait for daylight.

His decision made, Yoo-lah-teen returned to the woods and gathered fir branches. Then he felt his way back to the cliff. There he sat down, bent one branch, and fastened it around his head. He put another slightly longer one around his waist. Short boughs soon encircled each wrist, elbow, knee, and ankle. All braves about to attack an enemy must do this for protection; it was ancient tribal law.

Next Yoo-lah-teen dipped his fingers into the dried gourd tied about his waist. Inside it were war paints, both black and yellow. He carefully daubed his face and body as he had seen the warriors in his village do before going on the warpath. Now he was almost ready.

But he had yet to find a talisman, a charm. Something that he could carry to insure victory tomorrow. But what? It was too dark to see; and besides, what could there be in this dank, rock-strewn place?

To his surprise, one hand closed over something small and very smooth. There was just enough light for him to tell that it was a pebble, a bright yellow pebble! But how did it get here? Such bits of rock were only found on the beach.

Then at once he knew. One of the children Ish-me-ooth kidnaped had dropped that pebble, hoping a rescuer would see it. Perhaps Pay-koh had done it?

"My poor sister!" groaned Yoo-lah-teen, his face dark and angry beneath the war paint. Indeed this would be his talisman; he wanted no other.

It remained only for him to pray to the *Sag-hal-lee Tyee;* this he did, lying flat on his back, looking up into the night sky.

"*Hyas Tyee,* Great Spirit, grant to me the power to finish my task, to meet the Evil One and destroy her. Hear now my prayer. *Choo-hah,* Amen."

As if in answer the sky was suddenly filled with the wonder of the aurora borealis, the northern lights. Yoo-lah-teen had seen short rosy flashes at night before, but never anything like this. Long, vibrant streamers of purple, red, gold, blue, gray, violet, and green draped the sky, coming together in an arch overhead.

Yoo-lah-teen's mouth dropped open and his skin became gooseflesh. As he watched, the pulsing bands changed color, then changed back again. This continued for some minutes. Then, as if the universe could no longer contain such grandeur, the colors melted into pale rose-gray. In an instant even this soft glow vanished, and the sky was again all blackness and stars.

Yoo-lah-teen lay very still, puzzled by what he had seen and trying to calm his fear about tomorrow. For suddenly he seemed very small, and the island and Ish-me-ooth, very big. And the *Sag-hal-lee Tyee*, very far away.

He had a long time yet to think, since before any important event a brave must stay awake all night, planning, praying, gathering strength. This too was ancient tribal law. Yet for all that he was a wonder-child and determined to slay the *chehah*, Yoo-lah-teen was still just a boy. Clutching the yellow pebble, he slept.

IV

YOO-LAH-TEEN
PLAYS
A TRICK

The morning air was chilly. A cold mist rose from the river and drifted slowly upward in a thin gray veil.

Through it, Ish-me-ooth's great lodge appeared to dance up and down. Yet there was no mistaking the skin flap being moved away from its opening and a tall, gaunt figure emerging. Half-asleep a moment before, Yoo-lah-teen was instantly alert.

He flopped over on his stomach and pressed himself flat, trying to melt into the damp earth. When he was sure the *chehah* was not watching, he inched forward to the very edge of the overhanging cliff.

The witch, meanwhile, had reached the river bank. Wading in, she splashed about merrily, throwing cold water over her huge, blanket-covered self with a wooden basin she carried. As she bathed, she gradually moved out from shore until she was more than halfway across the river.

In order to keep watching, Yoo-lah-teen lowered his head and shoulders over the cliff. Ish-me-ooth was now almost directly below him. So near that, as she bent over to fill her basin, Yoo-lah-teen could see her hideous features mirrored in the calm water. Shuddering, he pondered what to do. Should he come out of hiding and face her now, or wait until . . .

Suddenly Ish-me-ooth stopped her bathing and stood still, staring into the water. Then she tilted her big head back and looked up at Yoo-lah-teen! He hadn't stopped to think that if her face was reflected in the river, his would be too.

"Come down, my fine lad, come down," the witch invited, licking her lips. Her voice was loud and shrill in the morning stillness.

Yoo-lah-teen was terrified. It was one thing, back in his snug village, to vow to rid the island of the *chehah;* it was quite another to actually be in her awful presence. He dug his fingers and toes into the earth and wished his body would stop quaking.

He had little time to think. Dropping her basin, Ish-me-ooth reached up one long arm and plucked him from the cliff. She set him on his feet beside the water.

28

"Well, my boy!" she roared. "So you've been spying on me! Where do you come from? Which tribe is yours?"

Yoo-lah-teen was silent. He was too afraid to speak, and anyway, he didn't intend to tell her anything. But how was he ever to slay such a *skookum*, such a mighty being? He fingered the yellow pebble, but only the *Sag-hal-lee Tyee* could help him now.

"Who are you? What is your name?" Ish-me-ooth persisted, digging her claws painfully into his shoulder.

"They . . . they call me . . . Yoo-lah-teen," he answered, still trembling.

The *chehah* gave a harsh, ugly laugh. "Yoo-lah-teen! The Wondrous One!" she mocked, studying him from head to toe. He was a bit skinny and wouldn't be very tasty until fattened up, she decided.

But right now Ish-me-ooth wasn't thinking just of her stomach. She was looking at his smooth bronze skin, without a blemish, at his shining black hair, his dark eyes, his white, even teeth. And she was comparing them to her coarse, pock-marked face, her dull, matted hair, her squinty eyes, and her yellow snaggled teeth.

Unable to restrain herself, she put out a giant hand to stroke his soft cheek. At once Yoo-lah-teen drew back and crouched, ready to attack.

Ish-me-ooth dropped her hand. "You are so handsome," she muttered, almost to herself. "Your perfect skin, your strong

29

features—how came you by them?" she asked, expecting no answer.

But Yoo-lah-teen had seen the strange look in the witch's eyes, and he thought he understood: she hated her own ugliness. If so, he knew how he could destroy the *chehah*. More sure of himself now, he stopped shaking.

"As to how I became so good-looking," Yoo-lah-teen began casually, "it's really very simple." He tossed the yellow pebble into the air and caught it. Ish-me-ooth's eyes followed his slightest movement.

"When I was just a little boy," Yoo-lah-teen went on, "my mother made me lie on the beach without moving for a long time every day with my eyes shut. And she put this yellow pebble on my forehead. A great medicine man gave it to her, saying it would make me handsome."

Ish-me-ooth thought about this for a moment. "Would it work for me?" she asked.

Yoo-lah-teen considered the question. "I should think so," he said with a shrug, flipping the little stone into the air again. Ish-me-ooth watched him as a cat watches a mouse.

Her natural impulse was to grab the pebble. But Yoo-lah-teen was quick; she had just seen that. He might throw the tiny stone into the river, where she would never find it. No, force was not the way. She would have to be sly.

"Will you sell it to me?" she asked. "I have many fine possessions. What do you want?"

30

It was on the tip of Yoo-lah-teen's tongue to offer her the pebble in exchange for any children she was holding captive in her lodge. But, if he let her live, she would just catch more. Besides, it would make her suspicious of him. No, he must not be so obvious.

Yoo-lah-teen held his head between his hands as if thinking hard. Finally he answered. "You can use it for a while, right now," he said, "and if it seems to be working, then I'll . . . I'll give it to you!" He forced a smile.

Ish-me-ooth stared at him, frowning. She didn't understand such generosity. But then she shrugged; certainly he had no further need of it. Anyway, she meant to eat him later.

Following Yoo-lah-teen's instructions, Ish-me-ooth stretched herself out beside the river. She folded her hands upon her chest, closed her eyes, and lay very still as Yoo-lah-teen carefully placed the magic pebble in the exact middle of her forehead.

"Now you lie there, and I'll just look around," he said solemnly.

Ish-me-ooth opened one eye and glared at him. Was he tricking her? Suspicious, she started to rise. But then she remembered that Nuck-ah-too, her lover, had told her the Indians had strange medicines. She lay back down.

"If I had but half this boy's beauty, how charmed Nuck-ah-too would be with me," she thought. "And I wouldn't have to chase children all over the beach. They'd run *to* me instead of away!" She closed her eyes and sighed, fanning the tall grasses nearby.

"Lie still," Yoo-lah-teen warned, "or the pebble won't do any good. I'm just going to climb back up the cliff and get some berries to eat. I'll be back when the time is up." He walked away slowly, whistling.

But once back in the marshy, boulder-strewn clearing he worked furiously. He heaved great rocks out of their resting places and rolled them to the edge of the cliff, lining them up one behind the other. Sweat poured down his face, smearing the war paint. It was very hard work, strong though he was, and he had to hurry.

From time to time he looked down at the witch to make sure she was staying just as he had left her and to call out encouraging words. "I think the pebble's taking effect," he shouted once. And, "Not much longer now," he said another time.

None too soon, Yoo-lah-ten pushed the last rock up to join the others. Ish-me-ooth was becoming restless. She twitched her arms, wrinkled her nose, and raised her eyebrows. Then, wondering at the silence—Yoo-lah-teen hadn't spoken for some time—she opened her eyes and looked up.

Yoo-lah-teen was not in sight, but he was watching. And as she started to raise her upper body—for her hunger pangs were such that she had decided to eat the boy at once, skinny though he was—Yoo-lah-teen sent the first boulder hurtling down upon her. Then another, and another, and another, and

32

another, until her screams grew fainter, then ceased, and her great cruel body lay motionless.

Yoo-lah-teen sighed with relief. Never again would anyone threaten to call Ish-me-ooth. Boys and girls might die, but they would not be torn apart, cooked, and eaten by the *chehah*. For Ish-me-ooth was dead.

V

A VOICE
IN
THE WOODS

As he half-ran, half-slid down the cliff, Yoo-lah-teen glanced at the sun and saw that it was just midday. That was good. He would have time to search the witch's house before dark.

Wrinkling his nose, he stepped across the *chehah*'s battered corpse, plunged into the river, and swam to the opposite shore. He scrambled up the bracken-covered bank and ran to the lodge. But just as he pushed the elk curtain aside, he heard a voice.

It couldn't be! Not here in the forest, where no Indian except himself had ever dared come.

35

Then he heard it again. It was faint, either singing or calling. But who could it be? He had better find out. It wouldn't take long, and maybe the person needed help.

Without another thought Yoo-lah-teen dashed into the dark forest beyond the lodge. Now that Ish-me-ooth was dead, there was nothing to fear. Nothing except her lover, Nuck-ah-too. But it was said that, though very dangerous, he was quiet and stayed hidden from view. Surely he couldn't be the one making the noise?

The farther Yoo-lah-teen went, the louder the voice became until suddenly it stopped. Instead he heard the slow, rhythmic tap . . . tap . . . tap of a hammer. Were there *two* other people in the forest?

After a time he came to a clearing. Here yarrow covered the ground like snow, and across the wide field of white blossoms huge fallen trees lay helter-skelter.

Over one log, stone hammer upraised, stood a giant! The tree trunk was as thick through as Yoo-lah-teen was tall, yet it barely reached the man's knees. He was cleaving the logs by using a great wedge hewn from *kla-toh-mupt*, or western yew, the hardest wood on the island. With mighty blows of his hammer he sank the tough wedge deeper and deeper into the somewhat softer tree trunks, cracking them open and—eventually—splitting them in half.

As the giant stretched himself to strike again, Yoo-lah-teen took a good look at him. He wore only a tight black loincloth

36

and was as rugged as the trees around him. Thick, muscular arms and legs ended in enormous hands and feet, while masses of snarled gray hair fell to his waist. His lopsided face—one cheek was lower than the other—was pale and expressionless. He had a hawklike nose and round, dark eyes that stared out from beneath heavy black brows. He had no chin, but from his wide, crooked mouth grunts emerged as he worked.

He was the hammerer, but who was the caller?

As if he read Yoo-lah-teen's thoughts, the giant stood still, wiped the sweat from his face with his free hand, threw back his head, and began to sing—a weird, spine-chilling half-yodel, half-chant.

Now Yoo-lah-teen knew that no one was in trouble and there was but one person in the forest besides himself—the ogre, Nuck-ah-too!

When the giant stopped howling and stooped low to examine the log, Yoo-lah-teen tiptoed nearer, close enough to see that the split was deep. The sides of the tree, forced a foot or more apart by the wedge, pressed tight against it; so tight that should the giant miss his aim and strike the wedge a glancing blow, it would fly out.

Still stooping, the ogre raised his eyes—and looked directly at Yoo-lah-teen! The boy's heart beat fast as he crouched lower in the weeds, and the giant's eyes widened in surprise at seeing an Indian in the forest.

"What a fine gift this boy will make for my sweetheart,

Ish-me-ooth," thought Nuck-ah-too. "He is slender, but she always says boy meat is tastier than girl, and she can fatten him up if she wishes."

As Yoo-lah-teen quivered, the giant studied him. The boy was alert—his bright eyes and darting glances showed that—and probably strong for his size. Nuck-ah-too sighed. He was tired and in no mood to chase anyone. Besides, he was very clumsy and the boy could easily outrun his long but lumbering steps. He would have to catch the young Indian some other way.

But how? As he thought, Nuck-ah-too tapped the stone hammer against his thigh, and it gave him an idea.

Yoo-lah-teen too was busy thinking. He had better destroy Nuck-ah-too before the giant found out Ish-me-ooth was dead. Otherwise Nuck-ah-too was sure to realize he had slain her, and there would be no place on the island, large though it was, where he could hide from Nuck-ah-too's vengeance. But how was he to do it?

Suddenly Nuck-ah-too raised his hammer, making ready to strike again. But as his arm swung down he opened his fingers, letting the hammer fall into the crack. Then the ogre grunted, shook his head, and turned to Yoo-lah-teen.

"Come here, boy!" he roared.

Yoo-lah-teen quaked but didn't move. Seeing his mistake, the giant smiled and said softly, "I'm so glad you came along, for I've dropped my hammer and can't get it. My arm's too thick. Come, fetch my hammer for me, that's a good lad."

Since he still had no plan for slaying the ogre, Yoo-lah-teen thought it best to do as Nuck-ah-too asked.

As the top of the log was level with the top of Yoo-lah-teen's head, there was only one way for him to get the hammer. He ran to the tree trunk, caught a toehold in its rough bark, and scrambled up. When he was over the spot where the hammer lay, he wriggled himself down into the split, head first. His legs waved in the air as he searched.

The ogre grinned.

Soon Yoo-lah-teen's arm touched the hammer. "I've got it!" he gasped, as his fingers gripped the thong that bound the stone to its wooden handle. "If I can only bring it up!"

The giant's grin broadened as he awaited the exact moment. Now! He raised his foot and kicked the wedge slantwise. It flew out, the sides of the log snapped shut, and Yoo-lah-teen was trapped, crushed to death.

Nuck-ah-too snickered and slapped his thigh. The trick had worked. He and his sweetheart would dine on roast boy tonight! He must yodel their secret tune to let Ish-me-ooth know she should build up the fire.

But midway through his long, queer cry the giant fell silent and stared at his feet. They were wet, for he was standing in a pool of water. Yet a moment ago his feet had been dry. Where had the water come from?

As he stared, sand trickled into the pool. Sand? In the forest? It seemed to be pouring from the bottom of the log, just under the crack. Just under . . . the body . . . of the Indian boy. Was the lad not dead? Was he somehow causing this?

Nuck-ah-too shook himself. He was imagining things. He was tired, that was all. Rest and a good dinner—he smacked his lips—would restore him.

But now the wet sand was rising! Nuck-ah-too blinked, but the mound was still there. And it grew until it was as tall as the boy had been. Then the pile dissolved and Yoo-lah-teen stood before him, hammer in hand!

Awe-struck, Nuck-ah-too backed away.

Yoo-lah-teen laughed. If only the giant could see the picture he made, cowering before a little Indian boy.

Hearing Yoo-lah-teen laugh, the ogre dared to speak. He was eager to apologize to this supernatural being.

"It was an accident," Nuck-ah-too declared. "The wedge just slipped out. It does sometimes, you know. I was sure you'd be killed, but you're alive," he marveled, looking the boy over carefully. "And with no broken bones—not even a bruise." Nuck-ah-too was very puzzled.

Yoo-lah-teen shrugged.

"I wish I could do that, turn myself into water and sand," the ogre went on. How amazed Ish-me-ooth would be, and on her bad days—when she didn't catch any children—he could escape her scolding.

41

Yoo-lah-teen shrugged again. Naturally Nuck-ah-too couldn't know about his strange birth. But then he had an idea.

"Oh, it's nothing," said Yoo-lah-teen. "Anyone can do it."

Nuck-ah-too looked doubtful.

"Of course you can," Yoo-lah-teen assured him. "You've just never tried. If I can do it, certainly you can."

The ogre agreed. Of course he could do anything an Indian boy could. Still, it was a trick, and he didn't know the secret. But maybe he could strike a bargain.

"If you'll show me how to do it, I'll teach you something," the giant said. "I'll teach you to sing!"

Yoo-lah-teen shuddered. He never wanted to make a noise like Nuck-ah-too, but he nodded.

First of all, the boy told the giant, he must drive the wedge back into the log, spreading its sides wide apart. Then Nuck-ah-too must put some part of his body inside the split.

"Just your hands will be enough," Yoo-lah-teen said.

While the boy watched, the giant knelt and rammed his hands and wrists into the crack he had made.

"Now you must look up to the sky and count," Yoo-lah-teen instructed.

Nuck-ah-too tipped his head back. "One . . . two . . ."

On the count of three Yoo-lah-teen struck the side of the wedge with all his might and darted away. As before, it sprang out and the sides of the log flew together, crunching to powder the ogre's bones.

42

The air was filled with the giant's screams and curses. He'd been tricked, and unless Ish-me-ooth came to rescue him, he'd bleed or starve to death.

"At last!" Yoo-lah-teen sighed happily as he hurried back toward the lodge. At last the *chehah* and her lover were destroyed, and the forest was forever free of evil.

But now he must try to find his sister, Pay-koh. He hoped he wasn't too late.

VI

INSIDE
THE WITCH'S
LODGE

As Yoo-lah-teen came out of the forest, the evening mist was rising from the river. The witch's big house appeared to float in the chill vapor.

Nearby a cowbird made its grating, rusty-hinge sound. In the distance a coyote howled. Overhead a killdeer cried forlornly. The hair behind Yoo-lah-teen's ears bristled. How he wished he were home, sitting beside the campfire, singing and watching the stars come out. But he couldn't go back until he was sure no children were imprisoned in Ish-me-ooth's lodge.

Eagerly Yoo-lah-teen shoved the skin covering away from

44

the high entrance hole and stepped down onto the earthen floor. When his eyes accustomed themselves to the gloom, he saw low blue flames above rosy embers that glowed like scarlet eyes in the blackness.

He walked toward the long fire pit. Beside it sat a cooking box, one large enough to hold a child. The box, very tightly woven of green willow wands, was filled with water. In the deep pit several white-hot stones lay among the ashes.

With a shudder Yoo-lah-teen realized that had he not slain the *chehah* and her lover he would be lying in that cooking box right now. And Ish-me-ooth would be dropping in the sizzling stones until he was boiled tender! His blood ran cold, and the hair on his head stood on end.

It was so quiet a sudden crackle in the fire pit made him jump. He turned around, squinting into the darkness. Surely there must be at least one child still alive? Just one the witch and Nuck-ah-too hadn't eaten?

By the dim light of the smoke hole Yoo-lah-teen could now see eight heavy posts supporting the long ridge pole. The posts were evenly spaced throughout the great lodge.

He walked toward the nearest one—and gasped. Lashed to it was a boy! He was fat beyond belief, and his head drooped onto his chest in sleep.

Yoo-lah-teen laughed and clapped his hands. But if there were eight pillars . . . ? Scarcely breathing, he peered ahead. Yes, he could see a small fattened body tied to each one!

45

He bounced up and down for joy. Eight children saved! And maybe, just maybe, his sister Pay-koh was one of them.

Yoo-lah-teen raced from post to post, tapping each child awake. "Ish-me-ooth is dead!" he called as he ran. "I have killed the witch! And the ogre too!"

But the prisoners, their eyes still covered with the gummy substance Ish-me-ooth had used, said nothing.

Yoo-lah-teen was puzzled. "Ish-me-ooth and Nuck-ah-too! They're both dead! You can go home. Don't you understand?" he shouted. But the children only cowered at the word "Ish-me-ooth" and tried to sink into the wooden pillars.

"Well, explaining can wait," thought Yoo-lah-teen. He searched around the fire pit until he found the witch's big shell knife, ground razor sharp and stained with blood. Then he hurried through the lodge, slashing the thongs that bound the children.

Suddenly he realized why they didn't understand him. They were from different tribes and spoke other languages. And they couldn't see who—or even what—he was. So, as he freed each child, he pulled the pitch from its eyes and acted out the slaying of the witch and the ogre.

The boys and girls hardly dared believe him. The *chehah*— dead! They had thought they were being released from the stakes in order to be cooked and eaten. But now their faces shone with joy, and their pitch-rimmed eyes sparkled. The lodge that had been so silent rang with happy cries.

46

Yoo-lah-teen beamed, sharing their bliss. But if only he hadn't been too late to rescue the children of his own tribe—especially Pay-koh, the sister he had never seen. Yoo-lah-teen sighed. "Oh, how disappointed See-tum-kah will be," he mumbled, and sighed again. Then he yawned.

He was tired and sleepy. He had better hunt for some mats or blankets to cover the children and then stir up the fire. It would be very cold before morning.

Groggily Yoo-lah-teen felt his way along one wall. But there was nothing there. He came to a corner and, as he turned, stumbled and fell across something big.

From it came a low moan! Instantly wide awake, Yoo-lah-teen felt the thing with his hands. It seemed to be a cage made of branches lashed together with vines. He peered inside but could see nothing. He poked a finger in—and something bit it!

Had the old witch kept a pet? He couldn't believe that. But there was something alive inside the enclosure.

Then a voice whispered, "Who are you? And why are those children laughing? There's nothing funny or happy here."

Yoo-lah-teen was stunned. A girl was speaking, and in his own language! Could it possibly be . . . ?

No, of course not. Five girls had been kidnaped that morning so long ago, and only one had escaped. It could be any one of the other four. He daren't hope—yet he clawed feverishly at the cage's fastening.

The small girl he pulled out was just as weak as the others —from lack of exercise—but she was thin, not fat. Quickly Yoo-lah-teen told her of slaying Ish-me-ooth and Nuck-ah-too. Then, his breath coming fast and his voice trembling, he asked, "What is your name?"

She was silent for a moment. Then, "My mother called me Pay-koh," she answered. Yoo-lah-teen shrieked and hugged her close, telling her that See-tum-kah was his mother also, and that she, Pay-koh, was his sister.

She laughed, then cried, then shook her head between her hands. Things were happening too fast! To calm her, Yoo-lah-teen asked, "Why are you not fat like the others?"

She sobered immediately. "I guess I was just lucky to be kept in this cage instead of being the *chehah*'s slave," she said. "I tried to escape so often that she tired of always chasing me and had Nuck-ah-too build this prison for me. And it's so dark back here, I could bury most of the food the witch gave me and stay thin. That's what saved my life for so long."

When the other children were asleep and Yoo-lah-teen and Pay-koh lay beside the fire pit, she told him about that spring morning on the beach, four moons ago, and how she had pushed a yellow pebble through a hole in the witch's basket.

"And to think my own brother found it and slew the *chehah* with it!" she exulted.

Soon, though, she slept. Yoo-lah-teen yawned and stretched. It had been a long day and he was very tired—but so happy.

He wriggled his toes and yawned again. "Tomorrow . . . we will all . . . go home!" he whispered as he fell asleep.

But it was many months before Yoo-lah-teen and Pay-koh returned to their village. She and the other children were too weak to walk very far, so Yoo-lah-teen had to pull them on the only thing he could find—the witch's long basket. Turned on its flat side, it made a sort of sled. But he couldn't cross the river or go up the steep bank pulling such a heavy load. He could only go across the island, coming out of the woods many days later, far away from his home.

And at each village where they stopped to deliver a child into amazed parents' arms, Yoo-lah-teen and Pay-koh were forced to stay for a month of celebrating. Each tribe wished to honor the young hero with numerous feasts and many rich gifts.

Thus the late summer months passed, then the Moon of Falling Water, and after that the Moon of Flying Ducks. Would they never get home, Yoo-lah-teen and his sister asked themselves.

But one rainy evening early in the Moon of Strong Cold Yoo-lah-teen, paddling a fine canoe given him by the last tribe, pulled close to shore. Ahead he could see three long-houses. Home! But would it, could it, be the same as when he left? He had seen so much and had such adventures, he just didn't believe that anything, anywhere in the world, had stayed the same.

50

Hurriedly beaching the boat, he and Pay-koh raced toward the village. Suddenly, though, Yoo-lah-teen slowed to a walk. Something was wrong. Dozens of dogs barked and ran to them, jumping and yipping. Yet not a person came out to greet them.

And then they heard it. The sound of voices, inside the lodge, singing the slow, sad Song of Death. Yoo-lah-teen and Pay-koh stared at each other.

"Who can it be?" whispered Pay-koh.

Yoo-lah-teen shook his head. He didn't know, but cold fear clutched his heart.

"Not . . . my . . . mother! It can't be!" Pay-koh cried. Dropping Yoo-lah-teen's hand, she burst into the lodge with him at her heels.

The Indians stopped singing and stared curiously at the two children. In the awkward silence, a subchief spoke.

"Who are you? Where are you from?" he asked kindly.

Yoo-lah-teen's mouth dropped open. Pay-koh gasped. But just then a short, plump woman ran forward and folded the two into her arms, laughing and sobbing.

"Pay-koh! Is it really you?" She held the girl at arm's length to examine her. "And Yoo-lah-teen! My son! Grown so tall and gone so long!" She wept afresh, clasping them close.

The other Indians gathered around Yoo-lah-teen and Pay-koh. "But we didn't recognize you!" they kept saying, their

51

bronze faces aglow at this seeming miracle. "You've changed so. How could we know you?"

And it was true. Pay-koh was nearly a year older, a bit taller, and now much sturdier. Yoo-lah-teen had grown several inches and, as a result of his labors, was hard and muscular.

"But how did you escape?" an old man asked.

"What about Ish-me-ooth? Where is the *chehah*?" asked a young mother, clutching her baby close.

"And Nuck-ah-too, the ogre? What of him?" inquired another.

Yoo-lah-teen held up his hand and called for silence. "We will tell you all about it," he promised. "But first tell us who has died. For whom were you chanting the Song of Death?"

The Indians looked at each other. Then the chief, a big man splendid in a long bark robe decorated with flashing abalone shells and wearing a hawk headdress, laid his hand on Yoo-lah-teen's shoulder.

"My son," he said in a deep, mellow voice easily heard above the crashing waves, "so many moons had risen and dissolved into the mists of time that we did not think to see you again. This ceremony—it was for you."

Yoo-lah-teen's eyes grew big. He hadn't thought of that, but, of course, it was what they would have to do.

"But now you have returned to us, alive and well," the chief was saying, "and instead of being sad, we shall have a great feast and do you honor."

52

So again there was the same eating, the same singing and dancing, the same gift-giving, the same recounting of how he had destroyed Ish-me-ooth and Nuck-ah-too. It was the same, yet it was entirely different. For this time he was home.

VII

YOO-LAH-TEEN SEEKS HIS VISION

Years passed swiftly and pleasantly. During the day Yoo-lah-teen fished, hunted, dug clams, made canoes, or netted flying ducks with the other boys. Nights, though, he deserted his companions to take a seat in the tribal council, the governing body made up of all the adult men. Yoo-lah-teen had been granted this honor despite his youth because of his great deeds. When he spoke in council—rarely, and only after deep thought—his elders listened to him with respect.

Although he was busy, Yoo-lah-teen found time to explore the forest. Often he went alone, to learn about the birds, ani-

54

mals, and insects living there. But most of all he studied the plant life. Each tree, shrub, or flower interested him, and he reasoned that even those without edible fruits should be useful to man. He thought much about this and asked the Great Spirit to teach him.

He thought, too, about the many sicknesses among his people. Being a wonder-child, Yoo-lah-teen had perfect health; but his sister, Pay-koh, and the other children suffered at times from sore throats, boils, and sick stomachs. Those See-tum-kah's age had fevers, coughs, headaches, vomiting spells, and other worse disorders. It seemed to Yoo-lah-teen that somehow the leaves, roots, or bark of the various plants might cure these ailments.

He experimented and found that valerian roots, ground to a powder, healed wounds, while partridgeberry tea speeded childbirth, and catnip tea helped colds. He learned that chewing yampa roots eased sore throats, and fresh, crushed leaves of blue flax applied to a sty cured it. The liquid from boiled rhododendron bark relieved an upset stomach.

Yoo-lah-teen spent long hours developing many effective medicines for his tribe.

One morning, as he pounded yarrow stems to put on a child's skinned knee, Yoo-lah-teen looked up to see the chief and his subchiefs approaching. What could be the reason for this unusual visit?

The chief spoke. "Yoo-lah-teen, you do not age as mortal children do, but it is our judgment that you are now sixteen, and therefore it is time for you to seek your Vision."

Yoo-lah-teen's eyes widened, but before he could nod, the men turned and walked away.

Yoo-lah-teen knew, of course, that at this age each male must go out and seek the particular spirit that would protect and guide him throughout his life. If the youth followed certain rules carefully for the proper length of time, his Vision would come to him. It would come in the form of an animal, a bird, a plant, a special cloud formation, or a voice crying along the wind—and grant him its power. It would leave him some token of its presence which he could show to others, and afterward he would be counted as a man in the tribe.

"And now I am old enough to find my power!" Yoo-lah-teen rejoiced as he bound the yarrow to the tiny girl's knee and dried her tears.

That very afternoon Yoo-lah-teen said farewell to his mother and sister and plunged into the forest. The medicine man and the subchiefs would follow him until he found the spot where he wished to stay. Then they would help him build a temporary shelter against wild or curious animals, see him installed in it, and leave. One seeking his Vision must spend four days and four nights alone, without food or drink. He was allowed only to smoke, to sing, and to pray. Should his Vision not come by the end of the fourth day, the young man

56

would return home, somewhat disgraced, to try again later. After four such attempts, he was permitted no more, but must spend the rest of his life with the women, helping them with their tasks.

Yoo-lah-teen hurried to the boulder-strewn clearing within sight of the *chehah*'s lodge where he had first seen the aurora borealis, the miracle of the northern lights. This, he felt, was the proper place for him to seek his personal Vision.

Hastily, the men rolled huge stones to form a square, gathered branches to cover them, and created a snug, safe enclosure for Yoo-lah-teen. They handed him a new pipe and a pouch filled with shredded red willow bark. Then they went home.

The hours crept by. When his stomach cramped in hunger, Yoo-lah-teen sang every song he knew. When his parched throat craved just one drop of water from the nearby river, he clenched his fists and prayed. When he feared that his Vision might not come and cold sweat bathed his forehead, he filled his pipe with the bark and smoked.

When he felt he could stand it no longer, he played a game with himself. What would his Vision be? And what would it mean?

Would it be the sleek wolf, meaning that he, Yoo-lah-teen, would always be thin, agile, and wily? Or would it be the bear, meaning he would be slow but have great strength? Might it be the sparrow, meaning he would have the gift of song? What would it be? The possibilities were as endless as nature herself.

At last it was the morning of the fourth day and still the Vision had not come. In desperation Yoo-lah-teen grabbed a sharp stone and hacked his hair—the sign of mourning or longing. Later he gashed his arms, legs, and chest, so that his blood flowed freely. More than that he could not do to invite his spirit power.

At the end of the long, long day, faint from hunger, thirst, loss of blood, and exhaustion, he lay on his back and, with a thickened tongue, whispered for the hundredth time his plea:

> *Holy Vision,*
> *Hither come,*
> *I pray you.*
> *Come to me,*
> *Bringing all your power.*
> *Oh, hither come,*
> *Great Vision,*
> *I beg you.*
> *Come to me,*
> *My life yours to rule.*

And suddenly, though it was blackest night, his shelter was lighted as if by the sun. In his waking, vivid dream an eagle soared! Yoo-lah-teen scarcely breathed, following the giant bird with his eyes until it was out of sight.

Then it was dark again. Too weak even to sigh in relief, Yoo-lah-teen slept until light from the real sun streamed into

58

his enclosure. Soon the medicine man and subchiefs would arrive with food and drink, to escort him home.

Yoo-lah-teen was very uneasy, for now he was sure that it had all been just an ordinary dream and not his Vision at all. Such greatness was not for him, and besides, no token of the visitation had been given him. Then, just as the men broke into the shelter and he raised himself, he saw it—at his feet lay an eagle's feather!

The men seemed as awed as Yoo-lah-teen himself. It was clear that his spirit power was that of the eagle. This meant that he had found favor with the *Sag-hal-lee Tyee,* the Chief of chiefs, and was himself destined to become a great earthly leader.

On the way home Yoo-lah-teen thought about this. If it was true that he was one day to be the chieftain of his people, then he should begin now to seek a bride. Not an ordinary girl but someone beautiful, talented, and able to advise him as he sought a better life for his tribe.

Where would he find such a wife? Since the *Sag-hal-lee Tyee* had looked kindly upon him, it seemed only reasonable to Yoo-lah-teen that he should visit his realm in the great sky yonder. In the kingdom of *Ill-hah-lee,* the land of eternal youth and sunshine where all good Indians dwell after they die, he would surely find the bride he sought.

But how to get there?

VIII

YOO-LAH-TEEN IN ILL-HAH-LEE

By the time he reached his village, Yoo-lah-teen's mind was made up. His bride should be none other than Tye-so-hee, the daughter of Nah-nah-hoop. Ugly and ill-tempered, Nah-nah-hoop was the doorkeeper of *Ill-hah-lee*, the realm of the Great Spirit. But Tye-so-hee was lovelier than any earthly woman. When she sang, her voice was more plaintive than a windflute, and when she danced she floated on air, graceful as a swallow in flight. She knew how to cure human illnesses, how to cheer the sad heart and calm the fearful one. All this Yoo-lah-teen had learned at his mother's knee; it was part of the lore of the

Salish tribes. Tye-so-hee was the one he would marry.

That night at the tribal council meeting Yoo-lah-teen told the other men of his decision.

"But you can't!" cried a subchief, aghast. "How could you get to *Ill-hah-lee?*"

"And even if you could," a tribesman said, "it's much too dangerous."

"Indeed it is," replied the chief. "That's why the lovely Tye-so-hee is still unwed. Nah-nah-hoop subjects any suitor to impossible tests, then slays him when he fails. If no young man living in *Ill-hah-lee* has ever won his favor, how could you?"

Smiling, Yoo-lah-teen answered, "I'm not afraid of Nah-nah-hoop. If I could destroy the witch Ish-me-ooth and the ogre Nuck-ah-too, I can outwit him. As to how to get there, I'll find a way," he assured them.

They argued far into the night, but Yoo-lah-teen would not be dissuaded. The next day he went to each man in the tribe and asked him to make arrows—long, smooth, very sharp ones—as fast as possible.

When, after four suns, a great pile of them twice as high as a man lay on the beach ready for use, Yoo-lah-teen called all the people together.

With his strong yew bow he shot an arrow straight above his head, far out of sight. It pierced the dawn sky at the floor of heaven and attached itself. Again he shot, the second arrow

62

catching in the notch of the first and remaining fixed. All morning long Yoo-lah-teen's bow bent and the cord twanged. By noon a slender chain of shafts reached from the beach to the land of *Ill-hah-lee.*

Yoo-lah-teen tugged at the chain; it held fast. Nodding in satisfaction, he dropped his bow and bade farewell to his sobbing mother, See-tum-kah, and his sorrowing sister, Pay-koh. Then, hand-over-hand, he climbed the rope of arrows.

Shielding their eyes with their hands, the Indians below watched as he grew smaller and smaller and finally disappeared. They were sure they would never see him again.

When Yoo-lah-teen reached the roof of the world, it parted, and he saw before him a fair land, much like the earth he had left. There were hills and valleys, trees and rivers, flowers and birds. But in *Ill-hah-lee* there was no morning fog, no chill rain, no howling gales, but everlasting sunshine and soft breezes. There was no sickness, no famine, no war, no slavery, no change. Life in *Ill-hah-lee* was always the same, and perhaps the day would come when Yoo-lah-teen, young and vigorous, would grow weary of this. But now he wanted to explore this new land and find Tye-so-hee.

In the distance stood a great lodge, something like the *chehah's.* About all Yoo-lah-teen could see were its housefronts, the deep bands of richly carved and painted wood attached to the upper part of the front of the building. They were

63

more beautiful than any he had ever seen. This, Yoo-lah-teen knew, must be the home of the dread Nah-nah-hoop.

But just in front of him were many fine mortuary posts, the emblems of death. Yoo-lah-teen stared at them, wondering if they marked the number of those who had sought Tye-so-hee in marriage. As he, Yoo-lah-teen, now sought her.

Determined, with his head held high, he strode up the path leading to the lodge.

Coming nearer, he saw two old women sitting before a campfire. In front of them was a single bowl of food they had just cooked and were getting ready to eat. As Yoo-lah-teen approached, one squaw cocked her head as if she heard something, but it was obvious neither saw him.

Realizing they were blind, Yoo-lah-teen all at once felt playful. He reached down and removed the steaming bowl just as one old woman was about to plunge her wooden spoon into it. Her mouth dropped open in amazement as she felt around with her other hand, but found nothing. Then her lips drew into a tight angry line.

Turning to her companion, she beat her over the head with the spoon, screaming, "I'll teach you to steal my duck chowder! You mean old thing! Give it back at once!"

The other squaw howled, "But you've taken my share, you selfish crone, you!" and struck the first woman in the stomach with her own spoon.

Yoo-lah-teen doubled up with silent laughter at these antics, but soon regretted his action. Replacing the bowl, he said, "I'm sorry for my little joke. Here's your soup. Eat and enjoy it."

Surprised, the two blind women turned their wrinkled faces toward him. "Who are you? And where are you from?" they asked.

"My name is Yoo-lah-teen," he answered, "and I come from an island in the blue waters far below *Ill-hah-lee*."

Now it was Yoo-lah-teen's turn to be surprised. At his words the squaws clutched each other and whispered together excitedly.

"Oh, Yoo-lah-teen, blessed is this day!" exclaimed one squaw. "For it was foretold to us aeons ago that when Yoo-lah-teen, the Wondrous One of the Salish tribes, should arrive in *Ill-hah-lee*, he would grant us our sight."

"Oh, please, please, make us see," begged the other. "We've waited so long."

While they continued to plead with him, Yoo-lah-teen considered the problem. This land was governed by the *Sag-hah-lee Tyee*, the highest Chief of all. If it was his decree that the squaws be blind, Yoo-lah-teen must not meddle. But they had said that he was the one who would one day restore their sight, hadn't they? Also, it seemed to Yoo-lah-teen that a good deed upon his entrance into *Ill-hah-lee* might be to his credit when he met the surly Nah-nah-hoop.

Yoo-lah-teen took up a sharp stick and bored a tiny hole in the middle of each old woman's forehead. Squealing with joy, the two of them looked upon each other and the beautiful land around them for the first time. At last they sobered and turned again to Yoo-lah-teen.

"But why have you come here? What do you seek in *Ill-hah-lee?*" they asked.

"I seek Nah-nah-hoop's beautiful daughter, Tye-so-hee, to be my bride," Yoo-lah-teen replied.

The squaws shrank from him, and their swarthy faces paled. "Oh, go back, Yoo-lah-teen, go back!" they pleaded in one voice. "No one can win Nah-nah-hoop's favor."

"He will never let anyone marry Tye-so-hee," one woman added. "Go back at once!"

As had the Indians of his tribe, the squaws argued and begged him to go no farther. But Yoo-lah-teen was determined and started up the path at a run.

"Wait!" called the fatter woman. "Because you have given us our sight, Yoo-lah-teen, we will give you something to protect you against all harm—even against Nah-nah-hoop," she added, shuddering.

"Yes, take these charms and keep them with you," said the other. Reluctantly Yoo-lah-teen held out his hand while the old woman placed in it a seed, a tiny feather, two twigs, and a little seashell. These were symbols of earth, air, fire, and water and the spirits that controlled them. He closed his fingers over the gifts, thanked the squaws, and again ran toward the lodge.

"Wait!" called the other woman. "Take this too," she bade him. "You will need it." And she gave him a stone hammer.

"It's very kind of you," Yoo-lah-teen said, grasping it with his other hand. "But you know," he said, smiling, "I have my own magic and won't need any of these things."

"Take them! And keep them with you! You will need them too!" the squaws insisted, their voices sharp.

Shrugging, Yoo-lah-teen thanked them again and hurried toward Nah-nah-hoop's lodge.

IX

YOO-LAH-TEEN MEETS NAH-NAH-HOOP

Directly in front of the lodge was a lake, its smooth black surface covered with a slimy green scum. As Yoo-lah-teen hesitated, his nostrils narrowing at the stench, the water rippled and a demon in the shape of a giant frog arose. It swam rapidly toward Yoo-lah-teen, then leaped at him. Its long sticky tongue flipped out, ready to devour him.

But the powerful jaws closed on air, for where Yoo-lah-teen had been there was suddenly nothing at all—nothing but a little pile of damp sand.

The demon-frog looked about with bulging eyes, croaked

piteously, then sank back into the water and disappeared. Yoo-lah-teen, an eager young man again, raced around the lake and up to the lodge entrance. He threw open the heavy outer doors.

Before him, guarding the inner doors and filling the passage-way, lay an enormous *soo-hah*, a salmon. Its mouth was open, and the cavern of its huge jaws so resembled a darkened room that Yoo-lah-teen started to walk in. He realized barely in time that the tall notched pillars weren't ivory, but the sharp teeth of a great fish. Just as the *soo-hah*'s mouth snapped shut, a pool of water—with a bit of sand mixed in—flowed past the salmon and under the inside doors to the lodge.

Himself again, Yoo-lah-teen was standing in the middle of a huge room. Facing him was the doorkeeper of *Ill-hah-lee!*

Yoo-lah-teen stared curiously at the stocky figure clad in a magnificent robe of sea-otter skins. Around his head Nah-nah-hoop wore a band of red cedar bark, and his left hand held a puffin-beak rattle which he shook in a steady roll. Above a wide mouth and sharp chin he had a razor-thin nose, so hooked no nostrils showed. His face was as colorless as mist on a winter's night, but fierce life glowed in the small dark eyes that stared at Yoo-lah-teen.

"You are in *Ill-hah-lee,* the Land of Shadows, and you have arrived ahead of your time," said Nah-nah-hoop. "Who are you and what is the purpose of your visit?"

70

"I am Yoo-lah-teen, and I wish to marry your daughter, Tye-so-hee," came the answer.

Nah-nah-hoop frowned, and his eyes became veiled as he observed Yoo-lah-teen's strong copper face and his tall, lithe body. Nah-nah-hoop sensed power in this earthling; perhaps he was the one?

The doorkeeper's frown deepened, then vanished. "If that is true," he said, "then you'll be willing to pass a simple test or two, won't you? So I can be sure you are a fit bridegroom for her? Tye-so-hee lived long on earth and is wise beyond mortal women. She knows the human heart, its passions, its fears, its joys, its sorrows, hopes, and dreams. The man who weds her must be worthy of such wisdom, grace, and beauty."

Yoo-lah-teen nodded.

Nah-nah-hoop clapped his hands to call his servants. "Build a great fire here," he ordered them.

Soon orange-red flames licked the ridgepole far above, and the intense heat spread to the very corners of the huge lodge.

"This is the first test," Nah-nah-hoop said, turning to Yoo-lah-teen. "Walk into the center of the fire."

Yoo-lah-teen paused. He was aware that Nah-nah-hoop was gloating, but what was he to do? This time returning to water and sand wouldn't help, as fire would quickly turn the water into steam and he would be destroyed. There was only one thing he could do.

71

Yoo-lah-teen clutched the old women's charms to his chest, hoped desperately they would work, and strode into the leaping flames. It was as if he stood in a cool, gentle breeze!

"Come out, Yoo-lah-teen," the *tyee* called, careful not to show his puzzlement. "You have mystic powers, and I'll be proud to have you wed my daughter," he said with a smile.

Yoo-lah-teen beamed. "May I see her now?" he asked eagerly.

Nah-nah-hoop frowned. "Not just yet," he replied. "I need your help with some work first. You don't mind?"

Yoo-lah-teen shook his head slowly. He was glad to help, but Nah-nah-hoop had many servants—why should either he or his guests have to labor? Was this another "test"?

"Just as soon as we've finished, I'll take you to Tye-so-hee," Nah-nah-hoop promised, laying his hand on the youth's shoulder.

His suspicions calmed, Yoo-lah-teen followed the door-keeper outside to the foot of a high, steep hill.

"We need more firewood," Nah-nah-hoop said. "You'll find plenty hereabouts. I'll go up to the top and gather some more."

Yoo-lah-teen's suspicions returned. He tucked his charms and hammer into his loincloth and set to work, but he listened attentively for any unusual sound.

He didn't wait long. Suddenly there was a great rumble and a gigantic log came crashing down the long hill. Before Yoo-lah-teen could jump aside, it was upon him—but it merely splashed through a small pool of water and sand, then rolled to a stop.

Far above Nah-nah-hoop listened impatiently for Yoo-lah-teen's screams and groans. There was only silence; the earthling must have been killed instantly. But just to make sure, Nah-nah-hoop sent a second log hurtling down the slope. Then, rubbing his hands and chuckling, he hurried back to the lodge.

Inside, he found Yoo-lah-teen waiting for him!

"You are crafty, Nah-nah-hoop," said Yoo-lah-teen, "but my powers are greater than all your guile."

For a few seconds the two men stared into each other's eyes. Then Nah-nah-hoop lowered his and said softly, "You have passed my tests and are worthy to wed my daughter. Lie here and rest"—he indicated a low couch of sealskins—"and I'll bring her to you."

As Yoo-lah-teen bent to lie down, the hammer fell from his loincloth. He picked it up, idly wondering why the squaw had thought he would need it. The tests were over now. Nah-nah-hoop had said so.

Or were they? A sudden thought crossed Yoo-lah-teen's mind. He struck the couch with the hammer. Something beneath it broke. Snatching the sealskins aside, he saw a dozen sharp, poisoned arrows attached to a rigid framework.

Yoo-lah-teen's patience gave out. Nah-nah-hoop was the doorkeeper of *Ill-hah-lee* and the deputy of the *Sag-hal-lee Tyee*, the Great Spirit, but he was also a trickster and a liar.

74

Furious, Yoo-lah-teen rushed after him, pushed him aside, and hurried into the small room Nah-nah-hoop had been about to enter. On a couch, asleep, lay a young woman.

At his step, she awoke. Yoo-lah-teen's heart jumped, then melted, for she was more beautiful than he had ever imagined! And Tye-so-hee arose slowly as if sleepwalking and held out her hands to him. She simply couldn't take her eyes from the handsome young earthling.

Nah-nah-hoop soon saw that his daughter's happiness lay in becoming Yoo-lah-teen's wife. Also, by now he realized that this young man was no ordinary mortal. It seemed best that he consent to the marriage, and he did so at once.

Amid great joy and festivity Yoo-lah-teen wedded the bride of his choice.

X

HOMECOMING

Yoo-lah-teen enjoyed life in *Ill-hah-lee*. He spent much time learning the ways of the Great Spirit, the many secrets of the realm of the *Sag-hal-lee Tyee*. These secrets he would reveal to his tribe when he returned to earth.

Delightful as the Land of Shadows was, Yoo-lah-teen had not forgotten his Vision. His spirit power was that of the eagle, and he would someday be the leader of his tribe. That was certain. But for now he was happy just to wander about *Ill-hah-lee* and spend pleasant hours with Tye-so-hee.

As time passed, though, Yoo-lah-teen found himself remembering more and more his island home, his mother, his sister, and the other Indians of his village.

He remembered the steel-blue waves topped with whitecaps. In his nostrils again was the sharp salt smell of the beach, and he shivered once more in a chill wind blowing dark clouds across an apricot sky.

He remembered the giant madroña trees hung with long gray lichen beards. He saw again shimmering dragonflies dancing above sweet-smelling thistles. In his memory he heard a red-shafted flicker's clear, liquid call.

He remembered the feasts held in his honor after he destroyed Ish-me-ooth and Nuck-ah-too. Again he tasted fresh fish blanketed with snipe eggs, salal berries, and seaweed, then gently cooked in rich *oolachan* oil.

Only Tye-so-hee noticed that instead of the merry tunes they both loved, Yoo-lah-teen played sad, haunting melodies on his windflute. She noticed and sorrowed, for she knew the time was near for him to leave *Ill-hah-lee*. She knew also she could not go with him. Her mortal life had ended, whereas his had merely been interrupted by his sojourn in the Land of Shadows.

On a fresh spring morning in the Moon of Camas Digging, when his tribe searched for the tasty root, Yoo-lah-teen said good-bye to his tearful wife and descended the chain of arrows.

Everything was as he remembered. Windrows of foam-frosted kelp and sea lettuce lined the beach, while drifts of orange paintbrush blazed against the dark green firs in the forest beyond. And, as he reached the ground, dogs came rushing at him, and people poured out of the longhouses to greet the stranger.

Yes, all was as usual—except that he didn't know anyone! Who was that plump squaw hurrying toward him, pushing four shy children ahead of her? And the old woman lagging behind, leaning on a sturdy stick? Who were they?

Just then the aged woman gave a shout of joy and tried to quicken her steps. "Yoo-lah-teen! Oh, Yoo-lah-teen! You have come back to us!" she cried.

That was his mother's voice! Then the stout woman with the four children must be . . . his sister, Pay-koh! He must have been gone for years, not moons! Yoo-lah-teen shook his head in bewilderment.

At See-tum-kah's shout the other Indians pressed forward. But instead of the slender youth who had climbed the rope of arrows, they saw before them a powerful, barrel-chested man, straight as a lodgepole pine, his every movement showing dignity and pride. His deep-set eyes held a faraway look, but they were kind, and his creased face smiled easily. He spoke with assurance, his voice deep and musical.

The admiring glances of Yoo-lah-teen's tribesmen seemed to say, "Here is the leader we've been waiting for!"

78

A subchief gave voice to everyone's thought. "You have come back just in time, Yoo-lah-teen," he said. "Our chieftain lies dying."

Thus what was destined to be came to pass. Before midday the old chief, See-tum-kah's youngest brother, died from battle wounds. As her son, Yoo-lah-teen would have been chief in his stead. He was now the rightful and worthy successor.

Then a strange thing occurred. At noon, without a cloud in the sky, it grew steadily darker. Most of the people were afraid, but the few who dared look up saw a faint circle of light around a black core. What was happening? Was the life-giving sun dying too?

Yoo-lah-teen calmed their fears. "I must tell you," he said, "that the sun and moon come out of Nah-nah-hoop's lodge every day. The giant salmon that guards the entrance tries to catch them as they pass by. Usually he fails, but once in a great while he succeeds. When he does, there is darkness on earth. You will see," he assured them, smiling, "in a short time it will be bright again."

It was as he said. Soon the eclipse ended and the sun shone.

Yoo-lah-teen taught his people many other things he had learned in *Ill-hah-lee*. First of all, he told them, they must stop their warfare with other tribes. The Great Spirit desired all men to live together in peace and brotherhood.

Over many years, through Yoo-lah-teen's leadership, his

79

tribe grew in reputation and in wealth. It became the greatest fishing, whaling, and seal-hunting clan in the region. The finest orators, the most skilled woodcarvers, the best musicians and dancers on the north Pacific coast were members of Yoo-lah-teen's tribe. And so peaceful was it that neighboring tribes sought its help in settling disputes among themselves.

Yoo-lah-teen's fame spread too, not only among the other island tribes but far beyond. All over the northwestern part of the great continent of North America, wherever Indians gathered, they spoke in awed tones of the heroic deeds of Yoo-lah-teen.

But now he was growing old and weary. His hair was as white as the surf that broke upon the outer rocks, and his hands trembled. At times his legs buckled beneath him. More and more he remembered Tye-so-hee, the gentle bride of his youth, and longed for the quiet and beauty of *Ill-hah-lee*.

His people sorrowed to see Chief Yoo-lah-teen's physical prowess gone, his mighty body wasting. But again he comforted them. "Do not fear for me," he said. "The thousands of stars that sparkle in the skies are all Indians who have died and now dwell above the earth. Soon I shall be among them."

He slept fitfully for many days. Then one midsummer morning he opened his eyes and called to his subchiefs. They crowded around Yoo-lah-teen's couch.

"I have had a vision," he said to them. "Even as I am speak-

ing a strange boat, a sort of huge canoe with white blankets attached to a pole, is entering our waters to the north. On it are men dressed in queer clothes and with very light skins. You will not see them. But others like them will come . . . many others.

"In the beginning they will do us much good," Yoo-lah-teen went on, his voice weakening. "They will bring us fine tools and a far better beast of burden than our dogs. But they will also bring diseases now unknown to us and a fiery drink that will gradually poison our young men.

"They will seize our land and call us savage when we defend it. They will make us promises, called 'treaties,' and break them, because they despise us. They will move us to 'reservations,' crushing our spirit utterly.

"Because we reject their religion, they will call us superstitious or heathen. Their social customs will be meaningless to us, and we will be deemed immoral. When we do not follow their rigid work patterns, we will be thought lazy and shiftless. Since we will revere our ancestral lore above their 'science,' they will say we are ignorant.

"More important, they will kill off our wildlife and pollute our clear-running streams; they will defile the very face of nature, insulting the Great Spirit. All this I have seen," Yoo-lah-teen said, his voice now a mere whisper.

With much effort he raised himself on one elbow. "Be

82

strong!" he warned his tribesmen. "Live in peace. And never let our ancient skills, our arts, and our sacred way of life disappear. Promise me!" he demanded, his eyes glittering.

They promised, and he slept again.

In the early evening of an autumn day in the Moon of Flying Ducks, an eagle circled the village a few times, then soared out of sight into the darkening sky. Yoo-lah-teen had returned to the Land of Shadows.

ELLEN TIFFANY PUGH was born in Cleveland, Ohio. She received her B.A. and B.S. in Library Science from Western Reserve University, and her M.A. in English and history from Northwestern University. She has been a librarian at various public and university libraries and now lives and works in Pullman, Washington. A member of the American Folklore Society, Mrs. Pugh has written several books for young readers, including *Brave His Soul,* a Junior Literary Guild selection.

LASZLO KUBINYI, who is well known for his children's book illustrations, was represented in the 1974 Children's Book Showcase and the 1974–75 AIGA Fifty Books of the Year Show. Among the many books he has illustrated are *Haran's Journey* (Dial) and *The Cat and the Flying Machine,* which he also wrote. Mr. Kubinyi is especially interested in Native American cultures and has done extensive research in order to illustrate *The Adventures of Yoo-lah-teen* accurately. He lives in New York City.